Secrets Aren't *Always* For Keeps

Meet
JENNIFER

Birthday: July 31
Best friends:
  Melody James
  Brenda Dubrowski
  Kay Lidcombe
    ("My Aussie pen pal")
Hobbies:
  Hiking in the woods
  Listening to my records
Sports:
  Softball
  Soccer
Favorite food (Yum!):
  Cinnamon toast
  Celery and peanut butter
Favorite subjects:
  Math
  Geography
  Music
Yuck!:
  Handwriting
  Hanging up my clothes
  My middle name: Esther
    ("Don't even mention it!")

Jennifer Hauser

THE KIDS ON THE BLOCK BOOK SERIES

Secrets Aren't *Always* For Keeps

Featuring Jennifer Hauser

Barbara Aiello and Jeffrey Shulman
Illustrated by Loel Barr

TWENTY-FIRST CENTURY BOOKS
FREDERICK, MARYLAND

Twenty-First Century Books
38 South Market Street
Frederick, Maryland 21701

Aiel

C-2

Printed in the United States of America

9 8 7 6 5 4 3 2

Book designed by Robert Hickey

Special thanks to David Lurio for permission to cite *Special Recipes for Special People*

Special Sales:

The Kids on the Block Book Series is available at quantity discounts with bulk purchase for educational, charitable, business, or sales promotional use. For information, please write to: Marketing Director, Twenty-First Century Books, 38 South Market Street, Frederick, Maryland, 21701.

Library of Congress Cataloging-in-Publication Data

Aiello, Barbara.
    Secrets aren't (always) for keeps: featuring Jennifer Hauser / by Barbara Aiello and Jeffrey Shulman; illustrated by Loel Barr.
    (The Kids on the Block book series)
    Summary: After successfully hiding her learning disability problems from her Australian pen pal, Jennifer becomes very apprehensive when her friend announces she is coming for a visit and wants to spend a day at her school.
    ISBN 0-941477-01-0
    [1. Learning disabilities—Fiction.   2. Pen pals—Fiction. 3. Self-acceptance—Fiction.]   I. Shulman, Jeffrey, 1951–
II. Barr, Loel, ill.   III. Title.   IV. Series: Aiello, Barbara. Kids on the Block book series.
PZ7.A26924Se   1988   88-24038
[Fic]—dc19

To the children who teach us about differences—
and similarities

CHAPTER 1

"Jennifer, do you have to keep doing that?" Mom asked.

I was so excited that I couldn't sit still. I was up and down, up and down. "I can't help it," I said, standing up. "These airport chairs are so uncomfortable," I explained, sitting back down. But it wasn't just the hard airport seats, and I wasn't just nervous. I was scared, too.

"I'll bet Kay is just as excited about meeting you," my Mom said. "It isn't every day you get to meet your very own pen pal." She straightened the barrette in my hair. "And certainly not a pen pal from Australia!"

She was right. My pen pal from Australia, Kay Lidcombe, was on her way to America. Any minute now, Kay and her mother would step off that plane to spend a whole week with us. I heard my Mom talking about all the things Kay and I could do on her visit, but her voice sounded tiny and far away. I was thinking about Kay.

We had been writing to each other for such a long time. We knew all about each other. We liked all the same things—music and animals and bike riding and especially sports. I told Kay she could play on the Woodburn soccer team when she was here. "Soccer?" Kay asked. "Oh, you know," I said, "what you call football." I remembered how hard it was to learn the different names for things they have in Australia—and how much fun it was to imagine what life was like there. I told Kay about everything: about my friends at school, about my favorite new song, about the boys I liked. And now she was here. Really here.

I felt sick. With an "umph" I slumped into the hardest airport chair in the world.

Mom was listening to one of those airport announcements you can never quite hear. "That's her plane," she shouted. "Just a few more minutes now!"

Just a few more minutes, I thought. Oh, just a few more minutes. "Come on, Jen," Mom said, sort of tugging me along. "Let's go to the gate where they arrive. What's the matter with you?" I was frozen in place. "Why aren't you coming? I thought you'd be so happy when Kay got here." Mom gave me one of her "What's going on here?" looks.

I *was* happy to see Kay. But I wasn't really happy. Oh, I don't know. What I really felt was all mixed up. My insides felt like they just got off a roller coaster. I wanted to see Kay so much. It would be so much fun to spend a week with her, to show her all my friends, to take her to Polotti's Pizza, to listen to my new albums. But what would I do about school?

You see, I hadn't quite told Kay everything about me. I never told her that I have a learning disability. I didn't tell her that I go to a special class at school. I don't know why I didn't tell her. Yes, I do. I was afraid. I was afraid she wouldn't understand. I was afraid she wouldn't like me because I was, well, different. I knew it was silly, but I couldn't help it.

I was angry at myself for not telling her right away. I had just made it a bigger problem than it really was. And I was angry at Kay—I don't even know why I was angry at Kay. And I was just about furious with these airport seats.

"Come on, Jen. Hurry up," Mom called.

Whoever thought that a pen pal from Australia would ever come to visit me!

CHAPTER 2

Maybe I should start at the beginning. I found Kay's name in the "Pen Pals in Need" section of the Woodburn school paper. How Kay Lidcombe's name got all the way from Melbourne, Australia to Washington, D.C., I don't know, but there she was in black and white. "I promise to write often," Kay said in the little description of herself in the paper. She promised to send a picture, too.

"This will be neat," I said to myself. "And hard." I really don't like writing letters, but having a pen pal from Australia—well, that was worth it! Not that I knew anything about Australia. I mean, I knew they had kangaroos, and koala bears, and something called Vegemite. I heard about that while I was listening to the radio. Someone was singing about the "Land

Down Under" (that's another name for Australia) and about eating a Vegemite sandwich. I didn't know what a Vegemite sandwich was, and it didn't sound too appetizing, but I liked kangaroos and koala bears a lot. So I figured two out of three isn't bad. I couldn't wait to write my first letter to Kay.

Dear Kay,

My name is Jennifer Hauser. I will be eleven on my next birthday, which is July 31. I go to Woodburn School, and I am in the fifth grade. I saw your "Pen Pal in Need" letter in the school newspaper. I would like to be pen pals with you.

I love to play sports. Do you, too? I play on the Woodburn soccer team after school and on Saturdays. We have boys and girls on our team, and I like to play goalie. Last Saturday our team won—and I had six saves!

I also love animals of all kinds. Do you have any pets, maybe a koala bear or a kangaroo?

Do you have rock music in Australia?

I will send you a picture as soon as the photos come back from the drugstore.

I was wondering. What is Vegemite, anyway?

Love,

Jennifer

That was my first letter to Kay. I couldn't wait to write it, but to tell you the whole truth, I didn't really, really write it. I mean, I thought up the letter and everything, but my best friend, Melody James, was the one who put it down on paper. She wrote down everything I said in her best handwriting. I just couldn't write it myself. You see, because I have a learning disability (LD, for short), sometimes I have trouble putting my thoughts on paper. Sometimes my words just don't come out the way they're supposed to. I wanted my first letter to be just, well, letter perfect. That's why I had Melody write down my thoughts. They were really my own thoughts, straight from my heart, so it wasn't like a lie or anything. How could I explain to Kay why I write the way I do?

It was a good plan. And it worked. I got a wonderful letter back from Kay.

Dear Jennifer,

Thank you for your letter. It was just bonzer to hear from you. I play football, too. Last week I scored a goal for my school team, running flat out when I did it. What a beaut!

Here is a picture of me. I hope you like it. You can see I'm a blue. This photo was taken at a barbie we had at the beach. Looks like I'm the only cacky hander in the group.

I love animals, too, especially my dog Rocky. I don't think koala bears or kangaroos would like to be house pets.

Of course, we have rock music here. This is Australia— not Mars, silly.

I can't wait to see the photograph you promised. By the way, what is a drugstore, anyway?

Love,

Kay
Your New Down Under Friend

P.S. Vegemite is like—well, there isn't anything quite like Vegemite. I don't know how to describe it. I wish I could just send you some.

Talk about being different! I was afraid Kay wouldn't be able to read my letter, and I could barely read hers. LD makes it hard enough for me to read, without figuring out these strange

Australian words. It sounded like a completely different language. Bonzer? And beaut? And cacky hander? I guess I had a lot to learn about Australia.

You know what I did? I wrote down all the new words in Kay's letter, so I could look them up in the school library. I kept a special notebook where I listed what all of the words really meant. I called it "Talking Down Under: How to Understand Australian Pen Pals." By Jennifer Hauser, of course. It looked like this:

Talking Down Under
How to Understand Australian Pen Pals
By Jennifer Hauser, Of Course

Kay:	Jennifer:
bonzer	awesome
football	soccer
flat out	fast
beaut	fantastic
blue	redhead
barbie	barbecue
cacky-handed	left-handed

I was so happy to hear from Kay that I read her letter over and over again. "My plan worked great!" I told Melody. I read Kay's letter to her, too.

My plan worked great, except for one thing. Kay was *too good* a pen pal. She wrote all the time. Of course, I loved every letter, I read them a thousand times, and I answered every one. Perhaps I should say Melody and I answered every one. And that was the problem. As Kay and I got closer and closer, our letters got longer and longer—and this was harder and harder on Melody. Poor Melody was a very important part of my plan. And Melody—well, maybe I should tell you about Melody.

CHAPTER 3

Melody James is my best friend. When I told her about my pen pal problems, she came to the rescue. She just didn't know what she was getting into. I still remember the fight we had.

"That's it! That's it! That's it!" Melody had had enough of my pen pal plan. "Jen, this is the fourteenth letter I've had to write. Fourteen! I've got a permanent cramp in my right hand. I'm glad you've made a new friend, but if this keeps up, you're going to lose an old one." Melody's patience had worn pretty thin.

"Listen, Jen," she said. Melody wasn't shouting now. "Just tell Kay about your learning disability. Sooner or later you'll have to tell her, and the longer you wait, the harder it's going to be. Why not tell her *now*? What's wrong with being different? Besides, if Kay is a real friend, she'll understand. So what if your letters are backwards. Who cares?"

"But maybe it's different in Australia," I argued. "Maybe they don't know about learning disabilities. Maybe they think kids who write backwards are weird. Maybe they'll think I'm from Mars!"

"Maybe," answered Melody, "and maybe not. You explained LD to me. Why not give Kay a chance?"

"I just can't. Not now. I just can't."

"And I can't keep writing letters for you. It's not fair."

"But you promised to help!"

"I did help. But how was I to know you'd find a pen pal who was a letter-writing machine? I have homework. I have piano lessons. And I have a permanent cramp in my right hand!"

Melody was heading toward the door. "I'm not doing it any more. That's final."

"Well, then," I shouted after her, "you can just find yourself another best friend, Melody Melinda James!" I didn't even watch as she stomped out. "That's what you can do," I said, mostly to myself.

"Friends," I muttered. I was angry, and I was afraid. I sat down at my writing desk and looked at the latest letter from Kay. It had arrived just this morning. I was always happy to get a letter from Kay, but today I didn't know how I felt. I opened it and just sort of peeked inside. I could tell Kay's handwriting a mile away. It looked bright and cheerful. It looked so neat. It just had Kay written all over it. And the letters were right every time. And the words were always right. "Isn't fair," I thought. I was a little bit ashamed of myself for thinking that.

Dear Jen,

    I haven't heard from you in a long time. I do hope all is well. Maybe you're knackered from too much school work? Or maybe the postie lost my last letter to you. Maybe the mail here is just crook?

    I hope you like this photo of me and my brother, Ian. It was taken last Chrissie. We were having a barbie at the beach.

    I don't mean to grizzle, but do write soon. It gets lonely Down Under.

                Love,

                Kay

P.S. Write soon.
P.P.S. Very soon!

Every letter Kay wrote made me smile. After I read each letter, I started a new page in "Talking Down Under." All the kids at Woodburn loved to read it. With each letter, the list grew and grew.

Kay:	Jennifer:
Chrissie	Christmas
knackered	tired
postie	mail carrier
crook	broken
grizzle	complain

But when I read this letter, only part of me smiled. The rest of me was confused. "Oh, now what am I going to do?" I asked myself. "Maybe Melody is right. Maybe Kay will understand. Maybe she won't even care. The kids at school don't think it's a big deal. I get special help in reading and writing, that's all."

I read Kay's letter again. I had to hold back my tears. I didn't want to get the letter all smudgy. "But what if she doesn't understand?" I wondered out loud. "And what if she does care? What am I going to do?"

CHAPTER 4

"About what, honey?" There was my Dad standing in the door.

"Oh, about nothing," I said.

"Let's see. What are you going to do about nothing? That's a tough one."

I could see that Dad was ready for another business trip. His bags were in the doorway. "I've got to run, Jen. Everything okay with you?" He sounded concerned.

"Oh, sure, Dad," I said. What was he going to do, anyway? Write my letters for me? Anyway, I already tried that.

"I love you, sweetheart. Left a message for you."

"Thanks, Dad. Love you, too."

Whenever Dad left for a business trip, he left a message for me on his tape recorder. The messages were usually pretty much the same: how much he loved me, and how proud he was of me, and how much he missed me when he was gone. They were kind of corny, but I listened to them over and over. I missed him a lot, too, even if he was gone for just a day or two. Dad was always there for me when I got sad about school, when it seemed like I would never learn to spell or write like the other kids. "Remember," he told me, "you learn differently. Not worse, not better. LD? That stands for learning difference." Yes, he was always there. "And when I can't be there," he used to say, "at least my voice will be."

I wandered into his downstairs office and plunked myself down into his big swivel chair. I loved to sit in that chair when Dad was gone. I guess it reminded me of him. It even smelled like him. I turned on the tape recorder and heard Dad begin his message. "Well, Jen, I'm off again. . . ."

For a moment or two the sound of my Dad's voice made me completely forget about Kay and Melody and my problems. I just thought how lucky I was. I kept thinking about what my Dad used to say: "And when I can't be there, at least my voice will be." I even said it out loud though I was the only one in the room. "And when I can't be there, at least my voice will be."

" 'At least my voice will be.' Dad, that's it!" I shouted. An idea was hatching in my head that was absolutely, positively, a stroke of genius. "My voice," I said. "There's nothing learning disabled about my voice. I'll send Kay my voice. I'll record my letters to her!" It was the perfect solution. I felt light as a feather. I spun around in Dad's chair till I made myself dizzy. I was dizzy with relief.

18

"Jenny the Genius!" I said, very proud of myself, "and no time like now to get started on Pen Pal Plan Number Two." I put a blank tape in the recorder and just let the words flow—no pen and paper to slow me down this time!

Dear Kay,

I know it's been a long time since I last wrote to you. I haven't been knackered, just busy at school. When your school year ends, ours is just beginning.

But now I have a better way of getting letters to you. What do you think of my voice? Do I sound American to you?

Thanks for the photo. Ian is a hunk—I mean, a beaut. Oh, whatever, you know what I mean.

I can't wait to hear from you.

Love,

Jennifer

Two weeks later I did hear from Kay. She wrote that she loved the tape. Her whole family listened to it, too. "Phew," I thought, "good thing I didn't say anything too personal."

"Maybe on the next tape," Kay wrote, "you could record some of your favorite songs." I was home free! My plan was just bonzer!

I even made up with Melody. I told her that her letter writing days were over. "That's a relief," she said. "So you finally told Kay about your learning disability. Good for you, Jen. I'm proud of you. Honesty is the best policy, you know."

"You're so right, Melody," I said. I tried to smile. What else could I say?

CHAPTER 5

I was home free—but only for a while.

"Jennifer! Jennifer! Guess what?" My Mom was shouting from the front porch as I got off the school bus.

"What did you do now, Jen?" Melody wondered.

"Jennifer, you won't believe it," Mom said, running up to me. She was even out of breath. She had a letter in her hand, and I thought maybe we won a million dollars or something. "Kay and her mother are coming here for a visit. They'll be here for a week. Can you believe it?"

I couldn't believe it. I mean, I couldn't even understand it.

"Huh?" I said. "Kay Lidcombe?"

"No," she said, laughing, "Kay, Santa Claus's wife. Why, of course, Kay Lidcombe. Her mother is coming here on business, and she's bringing Kay with her! Here, it's all here in this letter. And there's a note from Kay."

I couldn't believe my ears. I started to shout, too: "I'm finally going to meet Kay." I made myself read the note from Kay slowly—I didn't want to miss a single word—as I walked up the porch.

Dear Jen,

I'm coming to America. I'll finally get to meet you and your family and all of your friends!

It will be funny going to an American school when I'm on an Australian holiday, but I know I'll just love it.

Isn't this bonzer?

Love,

Kay

That note stopped me right in my tracks. I felt my insides climbing up the roller coaster—up and up and up. I heard an alarm bell ringing inside my head. It was ringing "School. School. School." Kay would be coming to school with me. "She'll find out," I thought. I felt like crying. "She'll find out I go to the Resource Room for special help. She'll find out I'm different. She'll think I'm weird. Who knows what she'll think? What am I going to do now?" I felt that roller coaster inside me stop for just a second at the very top. I looked over the edge. But it was too late now to change anything. I took a deep breath and marched into the house.

I had to think of something.

CHAPTER 6

I was still thinking as I waited for Kay's plane to land.

"Come on, Jen," Mom called. "Hurry up. Their plane is here!"

When I first saw Kay, her pretty orange hair, and her big backpack, I forgot about everything except that I was so happy to see her. When she said, "G'day, Jen" in her best Down Under accent, I knew it was really her. It was really Kay! Oh, we made quite a scene in the airport: screaming and hugging and carrying on. I began to tell Kay about all the things I had planned for her. My troubles were far away.

"Now, Jen," Mom said, "Kay and Mrs. Lidcombe are probably very tired. They've been flying for a long time."

"A corker of a trip, all right, Mrs. Hauser," Kay said. "I'm really knackered."

"Oh?" Mom said, looking confused.

"She means it was a long trip, Mom," I explained, "and she's pooped."

"Pooped?" Kay asked.

"I'll explain it to you on the way home. I have a lot to explain," I said. That was for sure.

So we took Kay and her mother home. I showed Kay my room, and we listened to records and talked about—well, just about everything—until we were just too tired to talk. "Kay," I said, as we went to sleep, "I'm happy you're here."

"Me, too, Jen."

I *was* happy. I still didn't know what I was going to do about school. If I thought about it, I could feel that old roller coaster start to roll. But I was happy, anyway. I don't know. Talking into the night with Kay (and sharing my room and sharing my secrets), I felt like I had a sister. I don't know how to explain it better than that.

Anyway, tomorrow was Sunday. So I still had twenty-four hours to figure out something—anything!

CHAPTER 7

When I heard Mom call, "Jen, phone for you," I just knew it had to be Melody.

"Jennifer Hauser, what do you mean? It just can't be." I was talking to Melody on the phone, but she was shouting so loudly it sounded like she was in the same room.

"Shhh. Not so loud. She'll hear you."

"Haven't you been writing to her?" Melody asked.

"Well, not exactly," I said.

"Just what do you mean, 'not exactly'?"

"Well," I said, and I told her all about Pen Pal Plan Number Two. "You've got to help me, Mel. Tomorrow's school."

"No way, Jen. You got yourself into this one, and you've got to get yourself out. It seems like you've been keeping a lot of secrets lately. Besides, what could I do? She can't stay here, you know."

"That's not what I mean. All you have to do is keep her busy while I go to the Resource Room. It's just for an hour."

"Just an hour? What am I supposed to do for an hour? Card tricks?"

"Just show her around," I suggested.

"And then what, may I ask?"

"I haven't figured that out yet. Please, Mel, be a pal. Oh, someone's coming. Got to go. Bye."

The "someone" who was coming wasn't Kay. It was my Dad. "Where's Kay, honey?" Dad asked.

"Oh," I said, "she's in the shower."

"How are you two getting along?"

I was just about to say "Fine" or "Bonzer" or something like that, but the words just wouldn't come out. Melody was right. I was keeping a lot of secrets lately. But I couldn't keep a secret from my father. It seemed like he could always see right through me. And I never really wanted to keep a secret from him. It never felt right.

"I haven't told Kay about my learning disability." There it was. I blurted it right out.

"And why not?" Dad asked.

How could I explain? I didn't really know the answer myself. How could I talk about that roller coaster inside me? "I don't know" was all I said.

My Dad thought for a while. "Oh, I think you do, Jenny. I think you know you're scared that Kay won't understand. The real question is, what should you do with this fear? Should you keep it bottled up inside you? Maybe you can even figure out a way so that Kay won't have to find out."

"If you have any bright ideas," I said, "just let me know."

Dad laughed. "But what good will that really do? It will just mean that you're keeping a secret from a friend. You know what I think it really means? I think it means you don't trust Kay. It means you don't trust your friendship. They say fear is like a lock on your heart. Open it up, Jen, and let Kay in." Dad stopped for a moment. "And speaking of the devil—"

Just then Kay came into the room, still wet from the shower and laughing and excited. "I, Kay Lidcombe, the great explorer of the Northern Hemisphere, announce an important discovery. In Washington, D.C., and Melbourne, Australia, the water flows down the drain in opposite directions! Astounding!"

I applauded and laughed, and Kay took a deep bow. I picked up the nearest pillow and launched it in her direction. We couldn't stop laughing. "And you know what else, Jen?" Dad said as he was on his way out the door. "They say that laughter is the key to that lock. Try it out."

Kay just looked at me. "And what was that all about?" she asked.

"Oh, you know fathers. They're just weird."

"Oh, I know," Kay said as she picked up another pillow and hurled it at me.

"Now, you're asking for it, Kay Lidcombe! Guest or no guest."

And the pillows started flying.

CHAPTER 8

That night, just before Kay and I went to sleep, I set in motion Pen Pal Plan Number Three. It wasn't much of a plan really, but I was fresh out of ideas, and to tell you the truth, I was tired of worrying so much. "Ten years old and I already have worry lines," I thought to myself.

"Are you asleep yet, Kay?" I asked after we had turned the lights off.

"Wide awake and ready for adventure!" she said.

"I'd like to play a game, Kay" I suggested. "It's a game called . . . called . . . Pillow Talk!" (Well, I had to think of something.) "Each person writes down one of their deepest, darkest secrets. Then you trade secrets. But you can't look. You just put it under your pillow. The first person to open the secret loses the game. See, it's a test of will power."

"You mean," she said, "it's a test of curiosity."

"That, too," I said.

"Well, if this is how they have fun in America, I'm game. When do we start?"

"Right now," I said and flicked on the light. I had worked up my nerve to get this secret out somehow, and there was no turning back. That old roller coaster was heading over the edge. Hold on to your hat, Jennifer Hauser.

I got out paper and pencil. Kay and I worked in separate corners of the room. We kept looking over our shoulders to make sure no peeking was going on.

"Are you done yet?" Kay asked.

"Almost," I said. Darn, I said to myself. Why does it have to take me so long to write? But I finally got it done, and I breathed a sigh of relief.

Dear Kay,
I want to tell you soemthing taht is so hard to say: I have L. D. which means ~~learnig~~ learning disaBility I larn in a differnt Kind of way. I go to a ~~spedle~~ special class for special help.
Love,
Jennifer H.

Finally, the secret was out. Well, not really out, but at least it wasn't completely inside. I stuck my note in an envelope and licked it shut. "Here you go."

"Now what?" Kay asked.

"Now what what?" I asked back.

"Now what do we do?"

"About what?"

"About the game, you dill."

"Oh, the game." I had to do some quick thinking. This was not exactly the best plan I ever had. "Well, now we put one another's secrets under our pillows and . . . and sleep on it. And in the morning we check to see if the secret's opened or not."

"That's it?" Kay sounded disappointed.

"That's it," I said. "Think you can sleep with my secret under your pillow?"

"Like a baby," Kay said. "But I don't think you can. I know you, Jennifer Hauser, and I know you'll be reading my secret before the lights are out."

"Not a chance," I said and flicked off the light. "See," I said, and I started to snore away. "Have a good night's sleep—if you can."

"Shhh. I'm already asleep," Kay said.

The way I figured it, Kay would never make it through the night without reading my letter. By tomorrow morning, the secret would be really out. And then I started to wonder about something else. I wondered what Kay's secret was.

CHAPTER 9

Monday morning came bright and early. I woke up before Kay and snuck a look under her pillow. I couldn't believe it. The letter was still unopened. So much for that plan. She just had to read the letter before I went to the Resource Room today. She just had to!

Kay came down to breakfast in good spirits. "Anything to report today, Jen?"

"I don't have the slightest idea what you're talking about," I said. "I certainly have nothing to report."

Then my Mom broke in. "Well, I certainly don't have the slightest idea what either one of you is talking about. But you'd better stop talking and start eating or you'll miss the school bus."

"That's not a bad idea," I thought. "Maybe that could be Pen Pal Plan Number Four."

"You should have an interesting day at school today, girls," Dad said between sips of his morning coffee. "What do you think, Jen? Kay will have a lot to learn." He smiled a knowing smile. "A lot to learn."

"Right, Dad," I said. "Would you pass the toast, please?"

Kay was a big hit at school. All the kids loved to listen to her talk. In fact, after just a few hours, everyone at Woodburn was walking around saying "G'day, mate." When I reminded them that I had made a list of Down Under words, I suddenly became the second most popular girl in the school.

While everyone else was watching Kay, I was watching the clock. After science class I was due at the special Resource

Room. I knew Kay brought my Pillow Talk letter to school because one of the rules of the game—I made it up at breakfast—was that you had to carry the secret with you at all times. I thought for sure Kay would have opened hers by now. But she hadn't said a word.

Lunch time brought a very close call, thanks to Melody. "G'day, mates. Mind if I join you?" said Melody as she sat down next to Kay in the cafeteria. I don't think she cared whether I minded or not. Like everybody else, her attention was on Kay. "So how's it going, Kay? Are you having fun yet?"

"I'm just having a bonzer time. Jen and I are playing Pillow Talk. I guess you play it all the time."

Melody gave me a very funny look. "Pillow Talk?" she said, a little puzzled.

I jumped right in. "Right, Mel. You know, Pillow Talk. You trade secret messages and see who reads the message first." Boy, was I nervous. "*You know*, Mel," I said. I gave her one of my best glares.

I think she got the point. "Oh," Mel said, "Pillow Talk. Of course. A very interesting game, isn't it?"

Finally the bell rang. Lunch was over, and for once I was actually looking forward to science class. I almost ran out the cafeteria door and bumped right into a very puzzled Melody. "Into the Girls' Room, Jennifer Hauser," she said. "We need to talk!"

"I had to think of something," I explained as Melody and I huddled in the bathroom. "Nothing went right. What else could I do? What if she thinks I'm retarded or something?"

"Well, she might," Melody said, "but if she does, she's making a simple mistake. Just tell her that LD is *not* the same as being retarded. Didn't you explain it to me? Well, if I understood the difference, I'm sure Kay will, too."

"I know. I know," I said, with a big sigh. "If only she'd open that letter."

Kay was a big hit with the teachers, too. Mr. Beame, our fifth-grade teacher, brought her up to the front of the room to talk about—what else?—Australia. "Did you know, Kay, that Australia is both the world's largest island and the world's smallest continent?"

"Of course," Kay said.

"Oh," said Mr. Beame, and we all laughed.

"Did you know, Mr. Beame," Kay asked, "that in Australia we have a special kind of turtle. Instead of pulling his head straight back into his shell, this one has to twist his neck to one side and sort of tuck it back into his shell."

"Well, no," Mr. Beame said, and we laughed again.

"Like this." And Kay twisted and turned and tucked her neck till the class and Mr. Beame and Kay herself were all roaring with laughter.

When the bell rang, most of the kids in Mr. Beame's class crowded around Kay to hear more about what Mr. Beame called "the mysterious and fascinating land of Australia." It seemed like a golden opportunity, so I just quietly made my way toward the Resource Room. "By the time Kay is finished answering questions about life Down Under," I figured, "I'll be finished with my special lesson for the day." I felt bad just sneaking off like that. But I didn't know what else to do. So much for Pen Pal Plan Number Three.

CHAPTER 10

I got to my work station in the Resource Room ahead of most of the class. I needed extra time for my Social Studies project, so I took out my headset and tape and found the book I was reading last week. It was all about cavemen and their paintings. They painted their caves with pictures of the animals they hunted. Somehow, though, I just could not pay much attention. I kept thinking about Kay and my secret. I even wondered if there were any cavemen who had learning disabilities. Would they paint the pictures of their animals backwards? Maybe the animals would be chasing them. I just couldn't help but laugh: "Meet Jennifer Hauser," I said to myself, "the learning-disabled cavewoman."

Just then I felt a hand on my shoulder. I turned around to say hi to Ms. Ricci—and there was Kay! In flesh and blood.

"I guess I lose the Pillow Talk game," she said. "I read your letter." I didn't know what to say. "I'm glad you told me. Did you think I was going to come a cropper because we don't learn the same way?"

"Come a cropper?" That was a new one to me.

"Fall apart. Go nuts. Lose it."

"I guess I thought—well, I don't know what I thought."

"What I think, Jennifer Hauser," she said, "is that friends shouldn't keep such secrets from each other."

"Well, you kept a secret from me, didn't you? Isn't there a Pillow Talk secret in this envelope?" I held up Kay's letter.

"Why don't you open it and find out?" she said.

That's just what I did. But it wasn't what I expected.

Dear Jen,

I know all about your learning problems. Your mother told my mother. I don't really know what learning problems are, but I do know one thing: secrets were made for friends to share. That's what friends are all about.

Love,

Kay

"You mean you knew all along! You let me ride this roller coaster all this time—and you knew all along!"

"Roller coaster? Jen, I think *you've* come a cropper."

"But why didn't you tell me?"

"I knew you'd tell me when you were ready. You can't force a secret out, Jen. It just doesn't do any good."

I felt like crying again—but this time because I was so happy. I introduced Kay to Ms. Ricci and showed her all around the Resource Room. Ms. Ricci told Kay about different kinds of learning problems and explained the use of the work stations. Kay even joined one of the learning groups. I was so proud of her.

What a day at school! It seemed like a long, long time, but at last the roller coaster ride was over.

CHAPTER 11

We all went to take Mrs. Lidcombe and Kay to the airport. Even Melody came along. "So the big cat's out of the bag, eh, Jennifer?" Mel said after Kay boarded her plane. The plane had pulled right up to the waiting area. I was hoping to see Kay one more time to wave good-bye.

"Yes, Melody," I said. "And the cat turned out to be a cute, little kitten."

"And Kay didn't run all the way home to Australia?" she asked.

"No, Mel, she didn't," I said.

Mel was about to tell me again about honesty being the best policy when my Dad saw something inside the plane. "What's that?" he asked. It was Kay holding up a sign. We all looked closely. We put our heads to the airport window. The sign read: "No More Pillow Talk."

"What's that all about, Jen?" Dad asked.

"Oh, you know kids," I said. "They're just weird."

Questions for Jennifer

Lots of my friends have questions about LD. Like these:

Q. What is a learning disability?

A. A learning disability means that someone learns in a different way from most people. Kids with LD may have a hard time learning some things in school. It might be in reading or writing or math. It might be in remembering things or in paying attention or in speaking clearly.

But it is also important to know what a learning disability is not. A person with LD is not stupid or lazy. People with LD are not slow learners. They just need to find their own way to learn things. As my Dad told me: "LD? That means learning difference. You learn differently, that's all. Not better or worse."

Q. Is there more than one kind of learning disability?

A. Yes. There are many different kinds of LD. My learning disability makes it hard for me to read and write. Ms. Ricci taught me the fancy name for it: "visual perceptual problem." I call it VPP. (I tell people that I'm a VPP—a very perceptual person.) It means I don't always remember things the way they really look. And sometimes it's hard for me to figure out how letters and sounds go together.

Let me give you an example. Look at this story and try to read it.

The Friembly Bog

Once ubom a tmie there was a friembl dobl. His name saw Jake. Jake belombeb to Bavig and Bhte. Davib and Beth aar tins. They ar nime yrse dol.

On e tome Jak went dow to the cellra. H was a ducket of soab. The tins wer doing to wsah the car. He liked some saop buddles out fo the ducket. When he darked, dig dubbles ca me out of hi s muth!

Last sum mre Jak founb a frenb. His frien sqw a tac named Freb. They blayde all bay. They nar aroumb and aroumbb tye yarb. Jake chased the tac ub te tre. Freb climbed up easily. Jake trieb t and trieb dut ehe slib back bown!

Not too easy, was it? Well, that's the way words sometimes look to me. Here's the story as you see it.

The Friendly Dog

Once upon a time there was a friendly dog. His name was Jake. Jake belonged to David and Beth. David and Beth are twins. They are nine years old.

One time Jake went down to the cellar. He saw a bucket of soap. The twins were going to wash the car. He licked some soap bubbles out of the bucket. When he barked, big bubbles came out of his mouth!

Last summer Jake found a friend. His friend was a cat named Fred. They played all day. They ran around and around the yard. Jake chased the cat up the tree. Fred climbed up easily. Jake tried and tried but he slid back down.

Here is another experiment you can try. Place an index card on your forehead and try to write the word "Zonker." Like this:

Now take a look at your work. I'll bet it looks pretty funny. That's what it's like for me when I write. I know what's right. And I try as hard as I can to make the letters come out right. But somehow, between my brain and the pencil, it doesn't work out the way it should.

Q. Do lots of people have LD?

A. Yes. And lots of famous people, too! Like Woodrow Wilson. He was a president of the United States. Like Thomas Edison. He invented the light bulb and the record player and about a million other neat things. Like Cher. I just love Cher! Like Einstein. That's right: even Einstein had a learning disability.

WOODROW WILSON

THOMAS EDISON

ALBERT EINSTEIN

CHER

Of course, most people with LD aren't famous. They're just like you and me. They're just trying to be the best they can be, no matter how they learn.

Q. What is a Resource Room?

A. My Resource Room is a special class where I go for extra help with learning skills. Ms. Ricci is wonderful. She thinks of so many different things to do that the Resource Room is always interesting.

This picture of our Resource Room shows the different activity areas. I work at each area. Let me tell you about them.

A. See the area with the tape recorders and headphones? Here we work to improve reading skills by listening to a book on tape while we read along. It helps me when I can use my eyes and ears together.

B. Another area is called "Special Recipes for My Special People." This is a little kitchen where Ms. Ricci helps us make our own meals. We use a neat cookbook that's easy for people with learning disabilities to use. It has both pictures and words for the recipes.

C. Ms. Ricci calls this our "In the News" area. Sometimes Ms. Ricci asks us to match news articles with their headlines. Sometimes we get to make up the headlines ourselves. That's lots of fun. Other times, Ms. Ricci will give us our "Word of the Week," and we have to find that word in the newspaper as many times as we can. That helps me remember how all the letters look.

D. This is the plant area. Here we grow different kinds of plants. Each plant needs a special kind of care, and we follow the directions written by Ms. Ricci. Ms. Ricci helps us read and follow the directions. I love this activity area because I get to take care of a living thing from the time it's just a little seed to the time it grows into a big and beautiful plant. It's like watching your child grow up before your very eyes! At the end of the school year, we have a special "Woodburn School Plant Sale." The sale makes money for Woodburn, but it's sad to see your children leaving home.

Q. How did you find out you had a learning disability?

A. That's a good question. I was having a bad time in school. I couldn't keep up with the other kids in reading and writing. What made it worse, I was trying so hard. Even my parents and teachers were confused. I was so good in some subjects. Why were reading and writing so hard for me? It got so bad I just didn't want to go to school anymore.

Finally, the Woodburn School counselor came to the rescue. She gave me several tests to take. That's how I found out I had a learning disability. It was upsetting at first. I didn't want to be placed in a separate class away from all my friends. I didn't really want anybody to know that I was, well, different.

But the counselor explained that I could stay in my regular class (with all my friends!) while getting extra help in reading and writing from Ms. Ricci. She said the tests showed that I was very smart. (I knew *that* all along.) And the Resource Room was definitely a step in the right direction. I began to see myself learning for the first time. I was proud of my progress—and happy to go to school.

Q. How did you get a learning disability?

A. No one knows for sure what causes LD. It's not something you can catch, like a cold or the measles. So you don't have to be afraid: I don't bark, and I won't bite. Maybe I could even teach you a thing or two.

Q. Is LD the same as being retarded?

A. No, it is not. Being retarded means that you are slow to learn. LD means you learn in a different way. It doesn't have anything to do with how smart you are. I have no trouble in some subjects. I'm "Jennifer Hauser the Whiz Kid" in math. I'm not slow to learn in reading and writing, but I don't learn the way most of the other kids do. That's why I get special help.

But I'll tell you one thing: all kids, including those who are slow to learn, are alike in feelings. Some people learn in different ways, and some people learn more slowly than others. But that doesn't make them stupid or weird or anything like that. They have no reason to be ashamed. I guess my Australian pen pal helped me learn that.

Q. Why did your letter to Kay look so funny?

A. Because the letters don't come out the way they should. Even if I try very hard, I sometimes have trouble remembering how they go.

It takes me a lot longer to read and write than it does most of the kids my age. I have to work hard at it. Sure, it gets discouraging sometimes, but I get lots of encouragement, too—from my family, and my teachers, and all my friends at school.

Q. Does it bother you if other kids tease you?

A. Of course, it does. Wouldn't it bother you? I just try to explain what LD is. I might even invite them to come to the Resource Room. But the way I figure it is, if they don't want to understand, if all they want to do is hurt my feelings—well, that's their problem, not mine.

Once, when I was feeling a little sad, I started complaining to my father. "Dad," I said, "I just can't do it. I'll never learn how to read. I'm just too discouraged."

"Discouraged?" he asked. "Do you know what word is hiding in discouraged?" I didn't know what he was talking about. He wrote the word "discouraged" on a piece of paper. Then he crossed out the "dis" and the "d." "What's left?" he asked.

It took me a little while to read, but at last I shouted: "Courage!"

"Courage. Enough said?" he asked.

"Enough said," I answered.

Q. How could you make a list of Down Under words if you have LD?

A. Surprise! There's lots of things I can do—LD or no LD. My learning disability doesn't stop me from reading and writing. I used my typewriter to copy the words from Kay's letters. That was easier for me than writing it out by hand. Mom helped me look them over in case I made any mistakes. And *ta da!:* Jennifer Hauser, budding author, writes her first book.

Q. Will you outgrow your learning disability?

A. Most kids don't outgrow their learning disability. But I don't plan to let that change my plans. I have to learn in my own way, but that won't slow me down. The important thing is to do the best you can, whatever way you learn.

About The Kids on the Block

Founded in 1977 by Barbara Aiello, The Kids on the Block puppet program was formed to introduce young audiences to the topic of children with disabilities. Since then the goals and programs of The Kids on the Block have evolved and broadened to encompass a wide spectrum of individual differences and social concerns.

Barbara Aiello is nationally recognized for her work in special education. The former editor of *Teaching Exceptional Children*, Ms. Aiello has won numerous awards for her work with The Kids on the Block, including the President's Committee on Employment of the Handicapped Distinguished Service Award, the Easter Seal Communications Award for Outstanding Public Service, and the Epilepsy Foundation of America's Outstanding Achievement Award. Her puppets have appeared in all 50 states and throughout the world. In addition, over 1,000 groups in the United States and abroad make The Kids on the Block puppets an effective part of their community programs.

For More Information

The Kids on the Block
9385-C Gerwig Lane
Columbia, Maryland 21046
800-368-KIDS

Association for Children and Adults
  with Learning Disabilities
4156 Library Road
Pittsburgh, PA 15234

Foundation for Children with Learning
  Disabilities (FCLD)
99 Park Avenue
New York, NY 10016

National Information Center for
  Handicapped Children and Youth
Box 1492
Washington, D.C. 20013

National Network of Learning
  Disabled Adults
808 N. 82nd Street, No. F2
Scottsdale, AZ 85256